Please, Papa

Kate Banks   pictures by Gabi Swiatkowska

Frances Foster Books
Farrar Straus Giroux
New York

Alice was making a farm

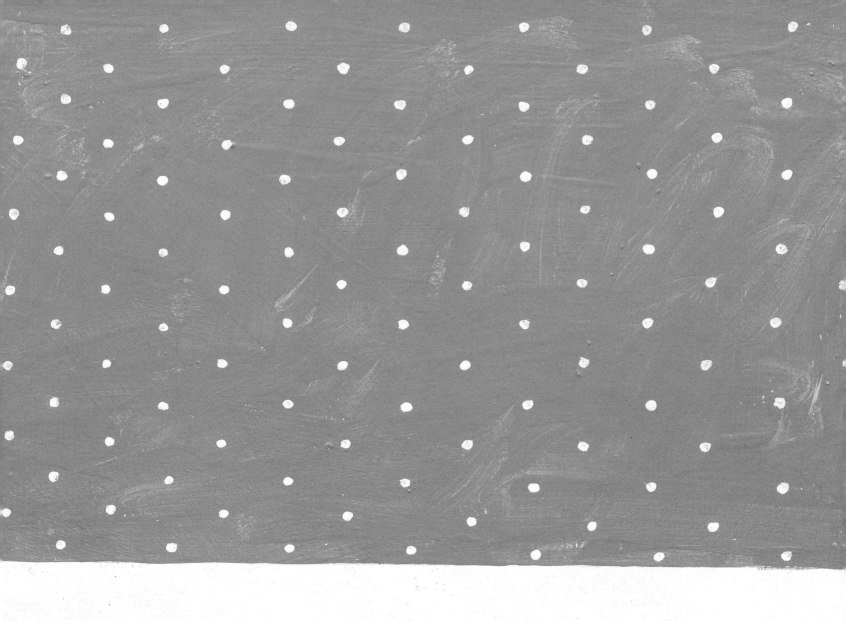

in the middle of her bedroom.

"Mama, give me the pig," she said.
"Say please," said Alice's mother.
"Please, Mama," said Alice,

and her mother

gave her the pig.

"Give me the chickens," said Alice.
"Please," said Alice's mother.
"Please," said Alice, and her mother
gave her the chickens.

Alice put them in the barnyard.
"Give me a horse," said Alice. "Please, Mama."

"I don't have a horse,"

said her mother.

When Alice's father came home from work,
Alice said, "I want a horse, Papa."
"I don't have a horse," said her father.
"Please, Papa," said Alice.

"Okay" said her father. He picked up Alice

and set her on his shoulders.

"Make the horse trot,"
said Alice. "Please, Papa."
Alice's father skipped
around the room.
"Make the horse neigh,"
said Alice. "Please, Papa."
Alice's father bobbed
his head and neighed
like a horse.
"Make the horse gallop,"
said Alice. "Please, Papa."
Alice's father raced
around the room with
Alice on his shoulders.

"Make the horse jump," said Alice. "Please."
"No," said her father.

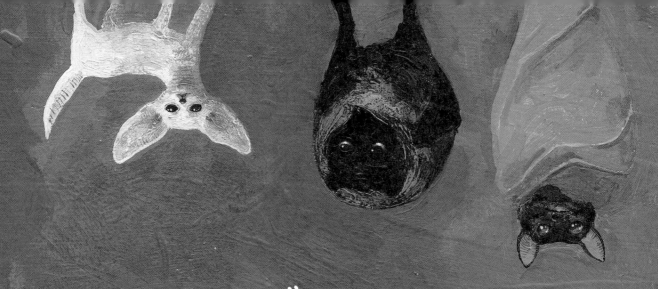

"Please, Papa," said Alice.
Her father shook his head.
"No," he said again. "This horse is tired."
Alice frowned.

Then the horse turned
and
looked at her.

"Alice, why don't you give this horse a rest?" he said.

"No," said Alice.

"Please, Alice," said her father. "Please."

"Okay," said Alice at last.
She climbed off her father's back.

Then she patted him on the head.

And while the horse was drinking
some water, Alice galloped back
to the farm to feed the chickens.

For Alice and Peter Von Theobald
—*K.B.*
For all the dads who know how to horse around
—*G.S.*

Farrar Straus Giroux Books for Young Readers
175 Fifth Avenue, New York 10010

Color separations by Bright Arts (H.K.) Ltd.
Printed in China by South China Printing Co. Ltd.,
Dongguan City, Guangdong Province
Designed by Jay Colvin
First edition, 2013
1   3   5   7   9   10   8   6   4   2

mackids.com

Library of Congress Cataloging-in-Publication Data
Banks, Kate, 1960–
    Please, Papa / Kate Banks ; pictures by Gabi Swiatkowska. — 1st ed.
        p.   cm.
    Summary: Alice learns the importance of saying "please" as well as
that this magical word will not lead to everything she wants.
    ISBN 978-0-374-36002-3 (hardcover)
    [1. Etiquette—Fiction.   2. Behavior—Fiction.]   I. Swiatkowska, Gabi, ill.
II. Title.

PZ7.B22594Ple 2013
[E]—dc23

                                                                              2012029533